The Three Words Project:
Short stories inspired by readers

Alex Hughes

The Three Words Project: Short Stories Inspired by Readers

Alex Hughes

http://www.ahugheswriter.com/contact-me

Or, email the author directly at alex@ahugheswriter.com.

Hughes, Alex C.
The Three Words Project: Short Stories Inspired by Readers / Alex Hughes
ISBN: (ebook edition) 978-0-9916429-7-7
ISBN: (print edition) 978-0-9916429-8-4

The author wishes to acknowledge the following professionals for their services during the production of this book, with great gratitude:

Developmental Editor: Bev Katz Rosenbaum, http://bevkatzrosenbaum.com/
Cover Designer: Scarlett Rugers, www.scarlettrugers.com
Formatter: Polgarus Studio, www.polgarusstudio.com

Contents

Introduction

In the summer of 2014, I asked the readers of my e-mail newsletter for just three words. The idea was that they would send me the words, I would choose the sets I liked, and I'd write flash stories from the those words and share them with the group. I was pleasantly surprised at how popular this was—I was sent dozens of sets of three words, some difficult, some easy.

Here's a small cross section of what they sent:

Dissonance, Invective, and Tactile – Lara
Echinacea, Surreptitiously, Haunted – Blanton
Alcohol, Tobacco, Explosive – Robert
Mariachi, Kendama, Express mail – Ricky
Azure, Mastodon, and Querulous – Michael
Rigor, Hemlock, Susurrus – Victoria
Beds Are Burning – Carol
Banana, Intermittent, Fedora – Lucene
Verbose, Absent, Rival – Alexander

And here are a few of the words my readers sent that I had to look up. (Well done, readers!)

Susurrus
Bouffant
Pareidolia
Caliginous
Esurient
Threnody

Simony
Excoriate
Psilocybin
Widdershins
Pard

I had so much fun writing stories from the words the readers sent. I had even more fun sending them out to the newsletter subscribers and hearing responses from the readers themselves. I found myself doing the Three Words Project again that winter.

The pages that follow are some of the stories from the Three Words Project, plus another two stories I'm excited to share with you from other projects. I've included the three words that inspired each of the project stories, and the inspiration behind the others, so you can see where they came from.

Oh, and before we turn the page and start the stories, if you'd like to participate in the next Three Words Project and read the latest stories first, sign up for my e-mail newsletter at http://bit.ly/AlexsList.

Enjoy!
Alex

Press One for Patience
By Alex Hughes

From a Three Words prompt by reader Ricky R. The words were *mariachi,* *kendama,* and *express mail.*

The twenty-third customer service call of the night connected just as all the others had, with a cheery voice proclaiming, "This call may be monitored or recorded for quality assurance."

The customer voice on the end of the line didn't wait. A large crash resounded through the unmonitored phone line. "What do you mean you sent me to a voice recording? What the [obscured language] kind of products are you [obscured language] selling these days?" Another crash, and the sound of a trumpeting dinosaur was picked up by the recorder.

The cheery recording continued, "Thank you for calling the Time Traveler's Help Line, sponsored by Megaton Temporal Products, your choice for the better time travel experience. The year is currently five thousand, eight hundred and four, B.C. For help in Twentieth Century American English, press one. For help in Ancient Sumerian, press two. For help in . . ." BEEP. "Thank you for choosing Twentieth Century American English. Please say your customer number now."

"Your [obscured language] company sent me a [obscured language] defective kit!" The sound of heavy breathing came over the line, along with the crunching of twigs and a huge crash. "Hah! Take that, you lizard! Think you can . . . . Oh, crap!" The sound of heavy breathing resumed, along with a low moaning sound. "He got up, how'd he get up after that?"

"Did you say, 'No customer number found'? Say yes or no."

"Yes, yes, [obscured language]!"

3

"Wonderful. We will connect you to a customer service representative presently. To help us serve you better, please tell us more about the nature of your issue. Press one if your time travel device has malfunctioned and you cannot return to your present time. Press two if you've accidentally caused a space-time rift due to a timeline alteration. Press three if—"

A BEEP and a series of obscured language words came over the line.

"I'm sorry. Zero is not a valid option. Press one now if you're in a life-threatening situation. Otherwise, press two to return to the main menu."

BEEP.

"Thank you. I am connecting you now. Thank you. Please hold."

A dinosaur roar came through the line, and the sound of a human scream. Then, the proprietary shake-shake-shake-cha-*boom* of the patented Mariachi Maraca Maldroiter™, and the strangled shriek of a lizard which had suddenly lost control of its limbs. A huge crash nearly overwhelmed the speakers of the customer service line.

The customer service team member stumbled over her words, then repeated, "Um, Time-Traveler's-Help-Line-this-is-Rhonda-how-may-I-serve-you, are you okay over there?"

Three shaky breaths came over the line. "No. No, I'm not okay. I've been running for my life from a T. Rex and three aviary things for the last hour. I'm exhausted, and I'm [obscured language]. Your stupid maraca thing didn't work until the dinosaur was less than two feet away. You're lucky I didn't get crushed in the fall—my estate would have sued, I can tell you that. Sued the pants off of you, too, if you know what I mean. You can't just send defective products with your time devices!"

The customer service team member took a breath, and in a move that garnered her high marks on later reviews, replied, "Are you in a safe place now, sir or madam?"

"It's sir, thank you very much. And yeah. The T. Rex is twitching, but it should be down for an hour or so if your [obscured language] product does half of what it's supposed to do. The aviaries are still circling, but they seem spooked." The computer system noted the incorrect use of 'aviary' in the record file, but failed to notify the customer service team member.

"Sir, I am happy to hear you are in a safe place. I'll need to get your customer number from you at this point."

A huge, frustrated sigh came over the line. "Yeah, whatever." The sound of rustling papers, and then the customer said, [redacted number].

"[Redacted number], is that correct sir?"

"Yeah. You'd better hurry, the flying things are eyeing me."

"What seems to be the nature of your emergency, sir?"

"Other than the peril to life and limb caused by your [obscured language] products? The wooden cup thing was supposed to keep this from happening!"

"The kendama, sir? The wooden handle with the cups and attached ball?"

"I wish you wouldn't say it like that, it sounds dirty. That thing is supposed to keep the local wildlife away from me. It's not [obscured language] working, okay?"

"Have you tried turning it off and back on again?" the customer service team member suggested.

"How the [obscured language] are you supposed to turn it off and back on again? And why in hell did you hide your technology in such stupid interfaces? It's the stupidest—"

The customer service team member received lowered marks for interrupting the customer at that point. "Sir, are you officially requesting a replacement of your Kendama Klearer™?"

"By express mail. Yes. Now, or you know, yesterday, when it would have done me some good."

"Sir, you know that Time Travelers Corporation has a policy against—"

"Yeah, yeah, just send the thing already."

A pause over the line, then the clicking of a keyboard as the customer service member appropriately checked the customer's history of mailings. "Sir, this is your third replacement within your personal timeline's past year. Express Time-Mail™ is extremely—"

"Yeah, yeah, whatever. I'll pay for it. Just send the damn thing already!"

The sound of tapping, tapping, tapping at the keyboard for three point seven five minutes—within one statistical variation of the average speed for the customer service team member's age and timeline position. A high whining sound came over the line.

"[Obscured language]," the customer yelled, over and over. Then he said, "Ow." The high-pitched whining sound stopped.

"Did the kendama arrive in good condition?" the customer service team member asked. She was docked points on this call for her informal phrasing.

"Yes. Ow! Ow! Get away from me you stupid birds!"

"Please turn on the Kendama Klearer™ by removing the ball from its spike," the customer service team member said. She repeated herself several times, while the sounds of an intense struggle came over the line.

Finally the customer came back on the line, with a whimper. "I'm hurt. You guys need to get me out of here! [Obscured language.] I'm going to have to do the whole [obscured language] mission again."

"Do you think you need a medical evacuation?"

"Yes! Get me out of here [obscured language]!"

"There will be an additional charge for—"

"Yeah, yeah, I'll pay it."

The sound of a clicking keyboard came across the line again, and the patented Siren Sound™ time team dispatcher sounded.

Medical personnel arrived within two minutes, local timeline, and retrieved a mostly-alive customer for dispatch to the Megaton Time Traveler's Hospital™. Customer care resulted in an increased customer revenue of 1.5g credits.

Customer service team member rated outstanding overall.

<<<<>>>>

Enigma and Maverick
by Alex Hughes

Written from a Three Words prompt by reader Adam R. The words were *enigma, resolute,* and *maverick.*

The two hundred and twenty-third annual meeting of the Society for the Advancement of Natural Magicians began with the usual announcements: magic workshop legalities, cauldrons for sale, giant rabbit employment bylaws, and the ongoing debate between the Moon-Driven Enigma and the Mighty Sun-Followers as to magical efficacy of various times of day. But, exactly thirty-seven minutes into the standard three-hour meeting, the proceedings were interrupted by an intruder.

Brunhilda the Ancient had just folded her knitting sticks and tottered down to the stage to reply to a particularly upstart Sun-Follower's protestations of the bylaws. She'd begun in a querulous tone, "I know you younglings under ninety feel that our traditions have become far too hidebound. How you manage to accomplish resolute Great Works without the necessary appreciation for—"

She was cut off by a puff of foul-smelling smoke roiling throughout the amphitheater. In the middle of a particularly dense patch of dark-blue smoke, a booming voice rang. "People of the Natural Magician's Society. You should know that I am here and I shall cut out your hearts with magic if you dare to deny me again!"

The smoke cleared, Brunhilda and all forty-three other Society members coughing on the foul odor. At the center of the smoke was a rat-like man with a pointy gray face and long tufts of ear hair. He was five feet tall at most, and that with stilts visible under his robes.

"Maverick!" an excitable magician in the back row cried out.

Another magician, next to him, shook her head in dismay. "He still owes me money," she complained, under her breath but still loudly enough that the entire hall could hear her.

A younger man named Zisor, sitting at the front, muttered, "What does he mean cut out our hearts? He couldn't cut out a heart with a knife and a diagram. Amateur." Zisor had always been a hothead.

"You are the amateur!" Maverick's face grew red with anger and he gestured with his long, pointy staff at the younger man. A flash of light erupted from the woman sitting behind him, and she disappeared. In her place was a long-nosed horned frog, the ridgy spines above its eyes giving it an angry look.

Magicians all around the transformed woman stood up, grabbing their robes and staffs. At the front podium, Brunhilda settled onto a nearby stool and watched patiently, her knitting needles clacking.

"You missed!" Zisor said, standing as well, puffing out his chest like a loon.

"You fool! You dare to challenge *me*? Me, the Amazing Maverick? I will laugh on your crushed bones!" The voice charm enhancing his voice failed at the last two words, so that, rather than the booming Voice of Doom he'd been using, "crushed bones" came out in a rather pleasant high tenor.

The crowd laughed.

Maverick swallowed, paused, and shifted the heavy necklace of spell charms around his neck.

Brunhilda adjusted her knitting, the shiny yarn between the needles catching the light so it seemed to glow.

"You must have paid a fortune for all the spell charms," Zisor said, in a mocking voice. "Too bad Squeaky-kins can't use any of them properly!"

"A duel," the crowd whispered to itself, and the magicians began filing out of the rows of chairs, to make room for the traditional circle.

"No!" Maverick gestured widely with his staff. Fire rained out, scorching the floor and chairs, and catching several magicians' robes on fire. One magician, stuck in the center of a row and unable to duck, disintegrated in cinders.

A gasp came from the crowd.

"Cheating!" Zisor yelled.

Brunhilda frowned from the front. "You go too far," she said.

"Fools, all of you! What does it matter if I cheat now? I will have my revenge!" Maverick yelled, and threw fire again.

One of the ancient wizards sitting beside the stage stood, hands out, the fire sputtering out halfway through its arc. Magicians cowered away, some now burned, murmuring to each other. The occasional spell was thrown at Maverick, but he stood firm, like he didn't feel a single one. Whatever he was cheating with was clearly incredibly strong magic.

"No self-respecting magician cheats on the circle!" Zisor said, trying hard to look unimpressed, but failing. His hands shook slightly until he wrapped them around his staff.

Another wizard stood, his knees creaking, and pointed his staff at Maverick. Pure magic streamed through the air, turning the path to ice. The magic stopped, as if it had never existed, a few feet from the upstart.

Maverick laughed, an ugly sound, and grabbed one of the spell charms. He started to grow, bigger and bigger, so big his head nearly touched the ceiling of the space. His stilts *cracked* and broke under the pressure of his now-massive legs.

Zisor took one look at the huge Maverick and fell back, quivering. "I concede!" he yelled in a pitiful voice. "I concede already!" He turned tail and ran out of the room.

Other magicians ran after him in droves, the crowd panicking. Brunhilda knit another row of shining yarn, the needles clattering so fast they sounded like falling rain.

All three wizards were now on their feet, throwing spells at Maverick.

"What fell magic have you, to hold against three wizards?" the second said, his old voice quavering with strain as he threw spell after spell.

Maverick lifted his staff in one mammoth hand, like a toothpick, and stepped with a *boom* and a *boom* forward, clearly enjoying the moment. "I applied thirty-seven times! Thirty-seven! And the last time you said I would never ever make it! After you let that quivering Zisor into the Society! Look what he became! Induct me now or I will kill you all."

"Never," the first wizard huffed.

"Our decision is final." The second wizard shuttered.

"Well, maybe we can talk about it after today," the third offered. The other two left their spells mid-cast and turned to look at him. "What? It's not every day we get an applicant who can terrify a group of the youngsters and hold us all off for a few minutes. He needs control, but I say we take him on."

"He's clearly using bought spells! That's cheating!" the first wizard hissed.

Maverick's voice charm came back in, and his voice echoed with a loud boom. "Really? You accept me? Really?"

"Absolutely not," the first and second wizards said at the same time.

"I said let's talk," the third insisted.

Brunhilda tied off the last of her yarn, now shining so brightly it hurt the eyes. Then she stood, her old bones creaking with the motion.

Maverick looked up, as if noticing her for the first time, just as she let go of the knitted piece.

Instead of falling to the ground, the shining square zoomed up and over, expanding as it went until it was a huge net, which fell on Maverick like a trap.

Suddenly he was small again, his voice normal, under a large, shiny rope net. "What?" he yelled. "What did you do?"

Brunhilda took up her clawed cane and slowly made her way down the stairs, ignoring his question.

Maverick struggled and cursed, but no matter how much he tried, he couldn't move more than an inch in any direction. One after another of his spell charms smoked as he touched it, and one after another failed.

"I was knitting that piece for my granddaughter to use in her hunting expedition," Brunhilda said quietly. "I am annoyed to use it so early. I will have to start over."

The three wizards, after a short conference among themselves, walked over to stand in front of the net. Brunhilda joined them in her own time.

"Well, boys," she said. "In or out?"

"Out," the first wizard said.

"Out," the second insisted, with a gesture across his throat.

"Eh, why not, in," the third said. "I still say it takes guts to do all of that to a group this large."

Brunhilda stood, unsteady, leaning on the cane, both of her gnarled fingers cupping the bulb of its top, her joints swollen with ancient arthritis. She regarded Maverick. Finally, she said, "I am sorry, boy. Working the spell charms does not make you a natural magician, and killing people is no way to make them like you. If you will reform, I will put in a good word for you with the Spellcaster's Union. But you must be good."

"There's a spellcasters' union?" The struggling Maverick stopped moving all at once, his eyes big.

On the floor, a small horned frog jumped over to stand below Brunhilda. Its eyes seemed to accuse Maverick.

"That's right," Brunhilda said. "Now, you have a lot of work to fix what you've broken. Best start now."

She lifted one gnarled hand, making a face like her digestion had failed her, and then the rope was gone.

Maverick pulled himself up.

"Eh, eh, eh," she said, holding up one finger.

Maverick deflated then, and looked at the frog. He sighed, and recited the spell to undo what he had done.

<<<<>>>>

Interruption of the Nap
A Tilde Lopez Story
By Alex Hughes

Written from a prompt from reader Lauren O. The words were *elephantine, perspicacious,* and *dirt.*

Tilde Lopez put her boots up on the desk and her hat over her face to block out the stripes of sun coming through the office blinds. It was daylight, afternoon to be exact, but she had been out late on a stakeout and needed her beauty sleep. She was getting tired of investigating cheating spouses in Sadtown, New Mars. It was better than working for the New Mars Police Force, that much was certain. No one was trying to kill her here, at least not yet. But watching idiots betray their marriage vows was getting old.

She had just dozed off, dreaming dreams of working monorails and on-time checks, when a loud *bang* shook her tiny office.

Tilde had her plasma pistol in her hand and pointed at the closed door before she was fully awake.

"Miss Lopez?" the dulcet sounds of her assistant came through the door.

"Did you overturn the water cooler again?" Tilde asked, keeping her pistol pointed at the door. That was their verbal code if her assistant was being threatened.

"Yes, ma'am," her assistant said, the all-clear.

"Then what's going on?" Tilde swung her legs down from the desk and pushed the pistol into the back waistband of her trousers. Then she sniffed, checking her shirt, then her armpits. Yeah, she'd have to shower soon, water tax or no.

"Um, There's a new client here to see you. You probably need to come

13

out here."

The office shook, *boom, boom, thud*, and then a shuffling sound came from outside.

Tilde sighed and opened the door, still wary. There in the main room she shared with three other service providers (all gone today, since it was New Mars Founding Day), was her assistant, and a . . . a very large nonhuman. A nonhuman standing in the middle of a pile of rubble, with a hole in the wall, and a broken door. Tilde frowned. She'd just gotten the door imprinted with "Tilde Lopez, Private Detective" yesterday. Wasn't it just like the universe to crash the thing now.

The nonhuman was a grayish creature, maybe six feet across, and thick, elephantine, with three long trunk-things coming out of its face. Its sides were covered in thick fur matted with dirt, and it smelled worse than she did. Despite this, it had two eyes that were surprisingly human, and it hung its head and bent its front legs in a gesture Tilde read easily as shame.

A low humming came from it, and then, a second later, the lights on the translator around its neck came on and an old-style British voice came out. "I apologize most sincerely for the damage to your doorway. I was attempting to knock, and then I lost my balance when the doorway broke. I am normally very lightfooted, I promise you."

"This building was intended for humans," her assistant said. If Lopez had said anything of the sort, it would have been offensive, but as her assistant was a multi-armed, pink, birdlike Derinki whose name Lopez could not pronounce, she got a pass. Mostly. "Your weight may not be supported by the beams," the assistant added. She spoke English just fine—when she wanted to.

"Too much of this world is intended only for humans," the elephantine creature's translator said, while the low-level humming continued, surprisingly pleasant, in the background.

"You'll get a bill for the door, and if you pay it, we'll have no problem," Tilde said. "You said you were a client?" A lot of PIs wouldn't take a nonhuman client, but she didn't care. She was bored with cheaters anyway, and they could prosecute her for breaking the Old Laws if they caught her.

Which they wouldn't.

"Yes. I am happy to be open with you. My name is . . ." and the translator cut out . . . "But you can call me Laredo. I am a . . . ." The translator cut out again and a peculiar pattern of rumbles followed. "But we will settle for Three-Trunk. I am certain my life is in danger. I want you to find the man who's threatening me and stop him."

"I'm a private investigator, not a bodyguard or a police officer," Tilde told him, though she was still licensed to kill; she hadn't let that one expire from the old days. She knew better. But protesting might raise the price of the job.

"No human bodyguard will take a nonhuman client, and the man who is threatening me is human, I believe. The police will likely side with him without more proof than I have. His messages are written in English on human style paper. They use slurs against my people specifically. I do not believe any nonhuman, except perhaps a Squibb, would use such language. And a Squibb could not manage the paper without shredding it. I do not know what to do. It is most distressing. At least, if you are involved, the proof will be listened to. You must help me."

Tilde thought this was a terrible idea, considering the threat to life and limb, but she'd learned to pay attention to her assistant. When she looked over, her assistant waved a wing at her frantically. That''s right—the accounts were low since they'd paid two fines last month. "I'll take the case," she said, then told him what she charged per day. When Laredo didn't react, she added, "Plus expenses and any fees we incur." If her life was going to be in danger again, she'd be well paid for it at least. Maybe her assistant would get off her back then.

"I hesitated to come to you, but you are rumored to be perspicacious . . ."

"Name calling will cost you extra," Tilde said flatly.

Laredo raised his trunks in almost a questioning pose. "It means well judged, clever. Is the translator not working adequately?"

"It's fine," Tilde said, defensive now. "When do I start? Also, we're going to need to talk about your life. A lot about your life. I'll need you to be completely open with me, and I'll probably have to talk to your family and business associates as well. It's going to be as invasive as hell if you want this to work." She half-hoped she'd scare the nonhuman off.

"I would rather not die," Laredo said. "I am happy to be open with you. What do you need to know?"

Damn. He was committed. At least the money was good. Now what? Normally Tilde would invite a client back to her office at this point. She looked at all the damage and decided to save her furniture.

"We'll do the interview here," she said. "For starters, who do you think would want to kill you?" Why not start with the obvious?

"I do not know for certain, but I stole about two million credits from my previous business partner to found my new business. I suspect he is behind this," Laredo said.

"I suspect you might be right," Tilde said. Anyone that came up with one answer that quickly usually was. "Tell me about the business."

"We sell personal grooming products for a variety of species," he said proudly. "Would you care to hear about our selections for female humans?" He peered more closely at her. "You are female, correct?"

She laughed. "Correct." Considering the dirt on his fur, she wasn't interested in anything from his store. She might as well finish up the usual questions, but she probably had what she needed. "Are you married or in a long-term relationship web?"

"Yes, I am established in a herd with several younglings. There are several complaints currently, but as the senior Three-Trunk has already executed one troublemaker, I don't expect they will be addressed any time soon. He is defensive since he is expecting a child soon," Laredo explained. "It is understandable."

"I'm sure it is," Tilde said, boggled. "Um, why did you steal the money? Did you ask first?" The translator sometimes got word choice wrong, and for something this important, she needed to confirm.

"I have heard this human saying that it is better to ask forgiveness than permission, and I acted accordingly. My former business partner did not react as I expected. I explained I would give the money back in two years, but it was already spent on the business. He said many cruel things, and the death threats started the next week. I need your help."

Tilde asked another question, and another, and her assistant occasionally added something she'd forgotten.

Out of the corner of her eye she saw movementand looked. There in the hall was a human. He was glaring at Laredo with true hatred. His head drifted down to a pocket.

Tilde went for her plasma pistol. She had it out and pointed just when she saw the gun. She shot.

The plasma hit the man dead on, burning through his chest. He fell over, shrieking, dead within seconds.

A horrible sound came from Laredo, and after a moment his translator sputtered, "Ouch. You hurt me."

Tilde looked. The heat from the plasma shot had burned a stripe down the fur of the nonhuman, who was now bleeding. Maybe the fur wasn't fur at all, but some kind of sensory coating that looked like dirty fur.

"Sorry," she said, without any real feeling. "Could you take a look at the human on the floor behind you please?"

She stayed well back as his feet *boomed* on the floor. As promised, though, he was light on his feet. His trunks stretched out towards the human, then dropped.

"Yes, I know him," he said. "That is the business partner at my last company, whom I stole from."

She held down her irritation. "Well, apparently he was serious about the death threats. Life lesson. You shouldn't steal from humans. They take it personally."

"I was always going to pay him back."

Her assistant chirped something at Laredo, who rumbled something back that the translator didn't touch. Hopefully her assistant was underscoring the don't-steal rule, though knowing her, there were some species slurs against humans in the mix. If it got the job done, Tilde wasn't in a position to argue.

She took a deep, deliberately loud breath to break up the conversation.

"Well, it seems I have solved your problem. I don't like killing people if I can help it, so I'll be charging you three days' expenses."

"Plus a kill fee," her assistant put in, clearly bothered though at whom, Tilde didn''t know or care.

"Sure, a kill fee, too. And a body disposal fee. I'll have a hell of a lot of paperwork taking care of this one."

"You hurt me," Laredo said.

"And I solved your problem at the same time. I'll waive the body disposal fee, I guess. Seems decent."

Her assistant trilled, but Tilde ignored her.

"You are a very fast worker," Laredo said. "I am happy to pay your fees. Do not fear, I will give you a very high recommendation with the Three-Trunks. You will have many clients from my people."

Tilde sincerely hoped not. Cheating spouses suddenly seemed a lot more attractive.

Even if she did like a little danger.

"Pay my assistant on your way out," she said, and went back to her office to see about that nap.

<<<<>>>

Thanks for Playing
By Alex Hughes

Reader Dr. Susan submitted the prompt words: *ferret, celebrated,* and *grotesque.*

The museum's lights were dimmed this time of night, and the assembled group of eight stood in the modern art gallery, their fine clothes fitting in with the exhibit. Three grown siblings and their spouses and children. None looked directly at the others, and tension was nearly visible in the air.

Matilda, a woman in her eighties, muttered something about inconsiderate young people, and seated herself on a small bench in front of a painting of a ferret.

"Why are we here?" Luke, her grandson at thirty years old, asked too loudly into the space. "You can't just hand us threatening cards and take us away from the party. Tonight was the night we celebrate the family's donation to the museum. Our very sizable donation. We deserve the party, and pulling us away from it is stupid."

"Be quiet, Luke," Matilda said.

He stuck out his chin, but didn't say anything more.

A balding man of about forty in a tattered tux walked into the exhibit room, moving with the assurance of a showman. "Thank you all for coming," he said, arms wide. "I am Sinclair, and I'm a private investigator. I called you here tonight for a very particular purpose."

A low murmur started in the back of the crowd, with the middle daughter and her husband. Neil, Matilda's son, a tall, greying man with the most expensive clothes in the room, took three steps forward. He held a wine glass in hand, and his attitude owned the room. "I didn't hire an investigator. You can leave now."

"Ah, but one of the family did. I was hired to ferret out the family's secrets." Sinclair pulled out a sheaf of papers from a coat pocket, fanning them out expertly. "I have here five years of e-mails from Neil back and forth to a waitress who goes by the handle Sherry Well Endowed. From the content of the e-mails, it's clear they've been having an affair at least that long."

The middle daughter muttered to her husband again at the back of the room. She clasped the small dog in her hands tighter, her face scandalized.

"Everyone knows that," Matilda said, almost bored.

"You didn't have to say it out loud!" Neil's wife exclaimed. She glared at Neil sparing the occasional disapproving glance at Sinclair.

Neil shrugged, not even bothering to look embarrassed as he put his hands in his pockets. His wife huffed and turned away.

The rest of the family pulled away from the couple. A teenager three feet away rolled her eyes, chewing her gum louder. Neil's daughter, Rose.

Sinclair frowned, as if he'd been expecting a more dramatic response. But he put away the papers and continued, "Of course, that wasn't all I found."

From the back of the room, the middle daughter gasped, the small dog she held making a small bark. "It was Vegas, okay? It was only the one time!"

Everyone turned to look at her. "What are you talking about, Lily?" Neil asked.

"The money I gambled from the savings account. It was only the one time. I've mostly paid it back," she wailed.

Next to her, her bored husband added, "And by mostly she means not at all."

"How could you?" Matilda's youngest daughter asked from the sidelines. "That's all of our money!"

"Yeah, that's our money," Luke, the grandson said in a resentful voice.

Sinclair cleared his throat noisily. "Well, you'll doubtless want to deal with that as well. That's not the secret I brought you all together to hear, though."

"And what is that?" Matthew asked, in a very irritated voice.

"Your grandfather's will—"

"Pappy Davis?" the youngest daughter interrupted.

"Yes, Davis, who made the family fortune," Sinclair said.

"Remember him?" Matilda said from her seat on the bench in front of the painting. "He worked his whole life, and now none of you even talk about him."

"We do so talk about him," Luke said. Rose rolled her eyes.

Sinclair shifted his weight. "As I was saying, I found incontrovertible proof that your grandfather's will was forged."

A gasp came from Lily—a gasp echoed by most of the crowd.

"Neil didn't get all the money?" Lily asked. "Not really? So he's been mean to me all these years for nothing?"

"No," Sinclair said, with all the dramatic delivery one person could pack into a word. "I found the original will. Davis left nothing to Neil, nothing at all. It all was left to his beloved wife, Matilda."

"I thought so!" Matilda tapped her cane on the floor for emphasis. "I thought so, you ungrateful children."

"You hired this guy?" Neil asked. There was an air of danger around him now, a tension that Sinclair reacted to by getting very, very calm.

"Yes, so what of it?"

"He's probably lying to tell you what you want to hear, That's what's of it. Nobody contested the will ten years ago, and you know why? It was a real will. There's no way he has proof." Neil held a hand in his pocket now.

Sinclair made a show of pulling at his nonexistent cufflinks. He straightened, in a showman's move. "Not only do I have proof of the will, Neil, but I've also done the work to find out that you killed Davis. He wasn't dying fast enough, so you forged the will and then you killed him."

"You killed Pappy?!" Lily shrieked. "You're grotesque!" Her little dog barked sharply in agreement.

"That's not even how you use that word," Rose said, with another eye roll.

Neil kept his hand in his pocket, looking around quietly. "You can't possibly believe this clown. Everybody knows you can hire somebody to say whatever you want. Mom is just grandstanding because she wants that house in Rio."

"I have proof, proof that will stand up in a court of law without any controversy," Sinclair said, with total assurance.

"No, you don't. There was—well, There's just no way you could have proof."

"Yes, I do."

"Fine." Neil brought his hand out of his pocket, bringing a small gun with it, a gun he pointed at Sinclair. "You tell me where the proof is and I won't kill you. Where is it?!"

Sinclair smiled. "You just gave it, in front of eight witnesses and myself. Thanks for playing."

"I told you he'd be an idiot," Matilda said.

Neil's face was red with anger, and growing more so by the second. "You—you can't do that. Don't you know who . . . I'll show you who's in charge here." He held the gun higher, and slowly squeezed the trigger.

Sinclair didn't move.

The gun clicked three times, loud in the silence of the art gallery.

Rose moved to the front of the room. "Unless you're planning to pistol whip the guy, give it up, Dad. I took the bullets out this morning."

"Thanks," Sinclair said to her. "I'll give you another twenty in a minute here."

"Make it a hundred," she said.

"Deal," Sinclair said, eyeing the gun.

"I—I—you can't . . ." Neil sputtered. "You can't do this!"

Matilda pulled herself slowly to her feet, leaning on her cane. "Well, sonny," she said, "I just did. I suggest you get used to it." And she walked out of the art gallery. Sinclair followed her out; he knew when to make an exit.

<<<<>>>>

22

Personnel Headache
a micro story by Alex Hughes

Words submitted by reader Corey F. were: *a bottle of aspirin, thunderstorms,* and *crow's feather.*

It's a dark night with booming thunderstorms. A small man pulls a lightning rod onto the roof to charge the experiment. A crow's feather whirls down from the sky, huge, as long as his arm. The man looks up.

Out of the sky, a crow descends, a dark mountain growing larger and larger as it hurtles towards him. Its massive claws grab the man, and it whooshes into the night. The lightning rod falls off the roof and crashes on the ground, broken.

Below, in the laboratory, the mad scientist sees the lightning rod splinter outside the window. He takes two aspirin from a bottle and shakes his head. Third one this month. How in hell is he going to get more personnel?

The crow killer gun will go another year without testing.

For the Birds
A Tilde Lopez story
By Alex Hughes

Written from a prompt from reader and blogger Stella Ex Libris. The words were *cinnamon, ticklish,* and *free-for-all.*

Tilde Lopez crept along a small crawlway, trying to get closer. Her latest private investigation case brought her to the Derinki aviary buildings, in the middle of the nonhuman quarter, and the damn birds didn't seem to understand adequate personal space. In a human neighborhood, she'd be squeezing through a real alleyway. Yes, there would have been dirt and trash and maybe some human waste, but she wouldn't be fifty feet off the ground on a small two-foot-wide accessway over empty space. With another of the things right over her stooped head, just ready to brain her. In her three decades of life, all on New Mars, she'd never been afraid of heights, but at the moment she was reconsidering that decision. The ground was a long, long way down.

Her knees hurt—too much pressure against the meshed accessway, even through her padded trousers—and her hands weren't much better, even wrapped in rags. Worse, the surroundings smelled intensely of cinnamon, what must be the Derinki waste, or a hormone used to mark their territory, or something. It was making her nose ticklish, and she couldn't afford to sneeze right now. Too much noise when she couldn't get caught.

She inched forward another few hands' breadths, and dislodged a small feather, which floated down, down, down, until she could no longer see it in the dim light. She looked away.

Tilde wrinkled her nose. Funny, in all the time she'd had a Derinki assistant, she'd never smelled this. It wasn't pleasant, this peppery cinnamon smell. Not at all. And the drop would be much less pleasant.

She pulled herself forward again, determinedly not looking down. Only another ten feet to go. According to her client, another Derinki, the stolen chestpiece would be in the window immediately ahead. She knew he was lying about something, but if it was a love quarrel, or an item she was stealing for him, well, she really needed the money right now and he wasn't likely to lie about location. She didn't like stealing, but she had plausible deniability, and that money—it had been much too long since her last client. She couldn't afford to be choosy.

The window would not be guarded this time of day, and the electricity shortages across New Mars would work in her favor, making it highly unlikely anyone would choose to spend the juice on a security system. Tilde would get in, get the decorative collar, get paid, and maybe take a day off.

Another strong whiff of that cinnamon smell, and she sneezed. She froze on the crawlway, waiting. Would any of the birds in the main flyway around the corner come investigate? She had her plasma pistol tucked into the back of her trousers, and that glass ball her assistant had given her with strict warnings in a case on her belt. She'd been too embarrassed to ask her assistant for anything other than a weapon that would work against Derinkis, given that she'd known better than to take the job. In retrospect, that had been a mistake. Her assistant was from this species after all, and might be able to get more information about the lie, whatever it was.

She sneezed again.

Two minutes passed, then three. No one came. Finally, Tilde shook off her nerves and kept crawling forward. When she reached the window, it was locked from the inside, naturally. Fortunately, she'd brought a small, powered prybar, which she set under the sill with some wiggle room before pushing the button to activate the powered pryers to spread. They did with a low hum.

The manufactured window-edging shrieked as it felt the strain, then *cracked* as the material gave way. The window itself moved open an inch, in a sudden jerk. Tilde reached for the prybar—

And nearly fell off the crawlway as a deafening alarm sounded. It blared in a high-pitched cacophony that literally stunned her.

Crap, crap, crap. Who in the hell would use the electricity on a security system this time of year?

Before she could recover enough to leave, three huge birds descended from the top of the building. One dove and caught her plasma pistol; Tilde felt the tug as it left the waistband of her trousers. She protested—

And found herself face to face with the sharpened beak of a Derinki twice the size of her assistant, and twice as cranky. A second Derinki landed behind her; when she looked back between her knees, he held a modified sonic pistol in one wing-claw, the pistol pointed directly at her.

Whatever was behind that window, she hadn't been sent here for a necklace. "Crap, crap, crap," Tilde muttered.

"Can you tell me where to find the consolate?" she attempted. Normally Tilde would have raised her hands, talked, and then run as fast as her legs would carry her away from this idiot case and her mistake. Unfortunately, this stupid crawlspace made that plan impossible. She wouldn't get two feet before she fell who knows how many stories.

"Nice try, human," the huge Derinki in front of her said. In addition to that ridiculously sharp beak that gleamed in the light (had he polished it?), his face held piercing eyes and a crest of red and yellow feathers she'd never seen before on a Derinki. He was also a great deal larger than she was used to; even with the vest she was wearing, that beak could do a lot of damage before she could move away. He told her: "Climb in the window, nice and slow. My boss will want to talk to you."

"Or what?" she said, before she thought about it.

The bird behind her cawed, a laughing sound.

The one in front of her tilted his entire head to the side. "Or we will push you over the side and see how well you fly," he said. Tilde noticed then that he didn't carry a translator-box around his neck; like her assistant, he had taken the trouble to learn English.

Which made her next play worth trying: "You won't kill a human, not in this part of town. It'll bring the authorities down on you harder than an anvil on a bad day. Let me go, and we'll call it a day."

He darted his beak towards her. She pushed back, almost falling. Her heart was beating all too hard. His beak had stopped, a millimeter away from her skin.

"You climb in the window or I get serious with you," he said.

#

Eleven minutes later, Tilde found herself handcuffed with rings intended for bird feet—extremely uncomfortable, thanks—and loosely tied to the only human-style chair in the building while a group of no less than five Derinki argued in warbles, doubtlessly about whether they could get away with killing her.

Tilde added the occasional comment to the conversation in English while she worked on getting the small wire out of her sleeve lining. The Derinki cuffs were already strained to the breaking point with her much-larger wrist bones, which made it harder but not impossible.

Ouch, she thought, knowing she couldn't say it out loud. She'd skinned one wrist on the harsh cuffs, but she'd finally gotten the wire. Even better, she'd found the opening to the lock with it, and was slowly working on picking the lock.

To the left, on the top of a high shelf near the circular door, sat the necklace-thing her client had sent her for. The day was looking up.

A nasty warble from one of the Derinki to the other—then an immediate response from a third, with strong body language. They were mad.

"No, really," she put in. "The New Mars Police Force has chemicals that will fluoresce with human blood, no matter how old it is or how often you clean at it. You really want them doing a routine check a few years from now and getting you on murder? There's no statute of limitations on murder, guys." The chemicals were an exaggeration, but only a slight one. She could mention that she used to be a cop and would eventually be missed as well, but that was likely to get them to stop arguing.

The largest bird spread his wings and mantled, big swooping

movements that took up the full attention of the other four birds. He said something short and shrieky in his native language, which Tilde didn't speak. They were probably debating killing her.

It didn't matter, though, because her little wire was doing the trick. Her wrists would hurt for days, but she almost . . . there. The lock clicked, and with an uncomfortable push, the cuffs came free!

Tilde was ready to go, and the idiots hadn't taken away her belt, or anything on it. She had the glass ball her assistant had given her, and the instructions memorized. She inched her hand over to open the pouch and take out the ball, small, quiet movements so she wouldn't be noticed in time to stop her. One small inch after the other. There.

She stood in one large motion, arms out like the birds', and threw the glass on the hard floor, where it shattered into a million pieces.

A sudden, overpowering smell came up, the same cinnamon musky thing she'd smelled in the alley but a hundred times stronger, so strong it made her eyes water. Also an orangy clove component, not that it made her eyes water any less.

She blinked back watery eyes, sniffed back the drainage, and stepped up with wide arms. She proclaimed, loudly and with the exact words her assistant had told her to say, "I'm a busy creature, far too busy for the likes of you. I will overlook your rebellion this time, but I will accept only one challenger to my authority at most in the next two molts. As I said, I am busy." Then she waited, heart beating too fast in her chest, to see what it would do.

Tilde didn't know what she expected. Three of the Derinki fell flat on the ground, cowering. The other two—particularly the large one—made a loud shriek.

"I do not accept your authority!" he said, far too loudly, in English. "You must fight me!"

But the other one hit him with a wing. "You cannot challenge the human! I will challenge the human. Why, those hormones must be artificial! This cannot be tolerated."

The first turned back to him. "And who are you to be the only challenger? Why, she probably doesn't even have the authority to set the rules! And I proclaimed it first! You are a half-bald pipsqueak and you are always getting in my way!"

The argument continued heatedly in the Derinki language, until the two leapt upon one another in a free-for-all of violence.

Tilde, thinking she needed to give her assistant a raise, stepped toward the door, retrieved the necklace from a high shelf, and left quietly. She'd been lucky . . . this time.

#

"You went *where?*" her assistant squawked, mantling her wings at Tilde while she sputtered in her native tongue. They were more or less on first-name basis, but Tilde couldn't pronounce her assistant's real name and they couldn't agree on an easier version yet, and given how angry she was right now, Tilde wasn't going to try a new version.

"I'm sorry, I should have told you the truth," Tilde said. "But I guess I knew I shouldn't have taken this one, and well, you do say you told me so a lot. I got out, okay? Your instructions worked like a charm. When is the client getting here?"

A rude sound. "Any moment. You're lucky that the ball worked—it shouldn't have. That building is the Ministry of Impulsion. You can't just go in there and bully them. And if I tell you I told you so, it's because you do stupid things like not talk to me about a Derinki client."

"I'm sorry, really. I won't be making that mistake again, trust me. What's the Ministry of Impulsion?" Tilde said. She took out the necklace she'd wrapped up and put in a pocket.

"Do you never listen to anything I say?" Her assistant bobbed her head. "That's the Derinki czar's own police here on New Mars. They can do whatever they want and even the human government can't say much."

Tilde paused midway through unfolding the necklace from its protective wrapping. "So they could have killed me after all?"

"For tresspassing on the czar's consolate? Yes, they could." Her assistant looked over at the necklace on the table. "You stole the chain of office?" A string of Derinki curses followed; Tilde knew how to order a beer and curse in about ten languages at this point, and recognized them. "You stole the [unpronounceable] chain of office? Why not paint a sign on your back and ask them to kill you? Honestly, if you die over this one, you will have deserved it."

Tilde sat down in her office chair, her stomach sinking in horror as she realized what she'd done. "We're in trouble, aren't we?"

A knock on the outside door, and her assistant went down to greet the client, the epitome of kindness. Tilde grabbed her backup plasma pistol from the bottom drawer and forced a cheerful smile. It wasn't a natural expression on her.

The Derinki client she'd met, a mid-sized yellow one with a small, blue crest who went by the human name of Jeff, was now accompanied by a larger human in a dark suit and sunglasses, a near-satire of a previous generation's government agent. Whoever he was, clearly, he wasn't government.

"We're here to collect the necklace," Jeff said.

Tilde looked at them both. "There was some trouble in retrieval." Her tone was flat. She didn't like this situation, with its constant change. "Turns out the building you sent me to was the Ministry of Impulsion. I don't like surprises."

"Do you have the necklace or not?" Jeff said.

Tilde looked at the two. She smelled trouble here, layers and layers of trouble that went well beyond a simple lie. Time was, when she was a cop with the New Mars Force, she'd have stuck her nose well into it, but she'd had the entirety of the Force to back her up. Here, now, she had only herself. "I have it, but it's not here and I don't want any more trouble," she said, with a glance to her assistant, who nodded. "Seems like I should return it to its owners and not ask any questions."

"You can't do that," Jeff said, too quickly. "You—"

The man in the suit took off his shades. "We're willing to pay double your stated price. You won't have any trouble from the Derinki."

"Can you guarantee that?" Tilde asked, keeping her tone level only with effort. Whatever was going on was getting worse and worse; if he was willing to overpay, this thing was probably lethal if it went wrong. She never should have taken the job.

"Well, no but—"

The man in the suit cut off Jeff one more time. "I can guarantee you'll have more trouble from us if you don't give us that necklace than you will from them if you do."

Tilde held his gaze in a long staring contest. She didn't want a shootout, not here, and she sure as hell didn't want a ground war with whoever was backing him. There was a time . . . but she was a PI now, she told herself, wings clipped, with her assistant depending on her. And this time she'd been the idiot. She looked away first. "Triple the price," she said. "Triple and you don't come back."

"Fair enough," the man in the suit said.

"You won't be hearing from us again," Jeff said.

"I'd better not," Tilde said. Her wings might be clipped, but it was still her PI firm.

The man in the suit pulled out an oversized moneyclip thick enough to contain triple her asking price for the job. "I assume cash is acceptable?"

Great. If he had that much cash on him, this really was bad. She'd done well to roll over, as much as it hurt her. Tilde nodded at her assistant to move forward to take the brightly-colored bills. The man wiped off his fingerprints from the clip before he handed the money over.

Reluctantly, Tilde got the necklace and handed it over, a sense of danger crawling up her spine as she watched them leave. Her backup plasma pistol sat in her back waistband uncomfortably, unused.

The door closed, and she and her assistant waited as the two clients left the building.

"I thought you were going to shoot them," her assistant finally said.

"I wanted to," Tilde replied. "But I'm too smart these days." At least that's what she told herself. She took a breath and turned.

Her assistant looked smaller, her head feathers slicked down with nervousness. Her wings were carried low, her head forward.

Tilde put a hand on her assistant's shoulder. "We got through it," she said.

"Yeah." Her assistant pulled away, but only after a moment.

"How likely is it that your people will come after me at this point?" Tilde asked.

Her assistant thought about that, head feathers coming back up. "I don't know. With that much hormones flying around, nobody's going to be thinking clearly. You got lucky you got out. Now? I don't know. If they didn't get you on camera, probably nobody's coming. Most of them think all humans look alike."

Tilde blinked. "Well. I guess that's comforting."

Her assistant pulled up to her full four-foot height then. "We'll take security precautions. I have some ideas."

"Great," Tilde said. "I'm hungry. Are you hungry?"

Her assistant blinked those big eyes. "Very hungry."

"Good. Then let's talk about your ideas over dinner. I'm buying," Tilde said.

"You don't have any money."

Tilde picked up her trench coat from the coat rack at the front of the main room. "We've got the cash from the client, and he overpaid enough for a meal or two. Thanks for saving my bacon today."

"You don't have any bacon," her assistant said.

"That's true," Tilde said, and held the door for her assistant. There was no discussion of where to eat; the only place in four miles to serve food they could both eat was in a small cave down the street. But it was hot. And they'd both survived today. "I feel like celebrating."

Her assistant stared at her. "Could you clean your skin first, please? You still smell like hormones."

Tilde laughed, let the door close, and hung up her coat again. "Sure, why not."

In the Realm of Hungry Ghosts
By Alex Hughes

Written from a prompt from reader Jude F. The words were *punctilious, saturated,* and *dour.*

The ground was dotted with the last spring frost, and with the sun barely up, the youths lined up for their coming-of-age *sidr*. Most already showed the beginnings of beards, all equipped with the best their family's armory could provide—ill-fitting leatherworks and bronze clasps, necklaces and helmets and sharp swords. The ones who would leave—and return—this day through the rite of passage would join the longboats to journey through the viking summer as men. Forever men, and worthy.

I, smallest and least, no true clansman as I'd been stolen from the Irish at six summers high, was to stay behind and prepare the fire pits for the sacrificial horse meat that would be cooked in celebration tonight. Instead I stood, with a helmet I'd filched from the midden and patched, a thin hide for a covering, and a rag about my head. In my hand, instead of brave sword or sharp axe, I carried a dull butcher's knife, sharpened so often its hilt held more air than blade. It was mine, even so, all I owned in the world.

As the priest stood before the saturated sunrise to chant the words of challenge and passage, I took my life and my fear in my hands and ran to the line, falling in next to the last boy standing to become a man. My heart beat wildly. The priest stopped mid-word, his ancient staff of power settling to the ground with a thud.

"What do you, boy?" he said. "This is the passage for those who would be men."

"I have fifteen summers," I said, though inside I quaked. "I have made the sacrifice and I wear the armor that is required."

My master, the warrior who'd stolen me away, yelled at me from a mile or more away. He would not be pleased. But I could not, would not live the life of a chattel servant any longer.

The priest looked at me. "You are a thrall."

"I am a boy of fifteen summers, and there is no custom against which you can bar me," I replied.

The priest frowned, dour with disapproval. "This is true, so far as I know, but, it is not wise."

"You will die in the crossing, Fool," the nearest youth scoffed at me. Erik, with a thick beard and armor especially made by the armorers for him, paid for by his father. The smartest and the strongest, he trained with the axe for hours a day. At less than a summer older than me, he was my better in every single way. At least here, in this place, where I was called Fool and no proper name.

And yet. Though I feared to the depths of my soul, though he was right, that I was too small and slight and weak to survive, neither could I remain as I was. My roots, my place—the place I remembered—was noble. Days I remembered what I had been while I scrubbed filth, with the insults and kicks abounding, those days were dark indeed.

"If I die, I die," I said, voice shaking. "I will try my fate and mettle even so."

"You cannot go," my master said from the sidelines, out of breath.

The old wise woman laid a hand on his shoulder, holding him back. She had been watching the scene from the beginning. "Be not punctilious with the custom. The Fool has one chance to prove his fate. Let him try."

Others spoke it among themselves, until the town settled on a conclusion, an answer, a yes. The priest raised his staff again. The ceremony began, and no more was said.

I stood, more and more afraid as the chanting went on. As the horse was led to the altar, I shook. Its neck became my neck, its death my assured death, and as the priest splattered blood on the line of boys and on my own face, I shook. I had been a fool, indeed, a fool as they had said. I would surely die on this fool's test. I would surely die, small and slight and weak, too stupid to know when to stop.

#

The other boys had the use of *faerings* or *karves*, strong boats from their family's stores, strong boats meant to take the fjords with their keels and laugh at the journey. Erik's small ship even had a dragon's head on its bow and stern, a fine and dread manner of transport indeed.

And I? I had a canoe, a log shaped and hollowed out over the long winter in secret, hidden away in case my mettle should hold and I should find myself here. It was a small and fragile thing, heavy in the water and small enough to capsize in a too-strong wave. Even my paddles were small things, my arms already aching just two hundred feet from shore as I fought with the waves, falling farther and farther behind the group as they unfurled their sails and settled into moving their larger oars in steady arcs.

Another day, my small canoe would have capsized, but as the sun was rising, the sea was calming, and though my arms burned I continued, paddling slowly as I went to meet my death.

I shook, but the shaking turned to another stroke of oar against water, as I made myself continue, heart beating, world turning anew. I would not, I could not turn back. My master would likely beat me to death from anger at my rebellion, and Valhalla was only for the brave, those that met their death in battle. If I was now to die, I would die with a chance at a death not a thrall's. But I did not want to die.

I held in sobs as I paddled, heart breaking with every stroke, but with every stroke knowing I could not return, would not return to be beaten and spat upon again. So I would go to my doom, and go with a song upon my lips. I sang, high and quiet, along with the battle song the others sang. Even so, I was a pretender, afeared greatly while others met their challenge with bravery. Even so, I remained, last and least, continuing on in my small boat and broken armor, continuing on, though my hands shook, though everything within me begged to turn back. I continued on.

Cliffs rose in front of us as we turned towards the forbidden fjord, the morning mist giving way to fog, real fog, fog that smelled of magic and sea and death upon swift wings. The song went on, through the fog, but as I paddled forward, the others faded—first the sight of their ships, then the sound of their singing.

I pulled the oar from the water, drifting forward, the world turning only to white fog. My lungs panted, from shame and fear and exhaustion. This was farther than I'd ever paddled before, and every muscle I owned—and some I did not—hurt, my hands developing long stripes of blisters against the rough paddle.

I could see nothing, no one, around. I took off my patched helmet, removed the rag, and wrapped the oar with it. The helmet thus sat on my head uncomfortably, but my hands could paddle again, before the blood came from the blisters and I could paddle no further.

I put the oar in the water again, moving forward through the thick fog. The only sounds were the lapping of the water against the canoe, and the sound of my breathing.

Then I saw it—out of the corner of my eye—the first one. A low green light in the fog, perhaps ten oars' lengths to the right.

I turned—and nearly capsized. I righted myself, heart beating, the canoe still bobbing unsteadily. The light was gone, but I knew what I'd seen.

All the old stories of hungry ghosts in the darkness came back, the will o' wisps, the pookas, the dark elves, the fell mermaids and more who waited to steal the breath from a man and consign him to the deep. No man would tell of what he had seen in the crossing, and my mind raced with horrible possibilities.

Another light, a red light, to the left, that disappeared as soon as my eye landed upon it. Then another, green, to the front.

I yelped as one appeared in front of me. Then it was gone.

The canoe shook as I did, afeared.

"Show yourself!" I called to the creature, the spirit, the hungry ghost. "If you would consume my soul, I must see you first."

Long lines of light illuminated the edge of the fog, almost too far to see.

Then they came closer, and closer, a pace at a time. My heart quaked within me, my fear pinning me in place like a rabbit before an attacking hawk.

I breathed, forcing myself to move, to think, as I did when my master was in a foul mood and inclined to beat me. Sometimes if I thought, if I was clever, I could get away. Sometimes my small arms were enough to pull me into a tree, away from the screaming, or my thin legs enough to run away. My master was slow and lazy. Though my heart beat as the lights grew closer, though I breathed like I was sure to die, they were not here yet. Perhaps I could row away, or swim away.

I pulled the oar into my lap, uncaring of the wetness. With shaking hand, I slowly retrieved my thin-bladed knife. What manner of creature would I face? What dread spirits were in these lights?

A low keening sound came from them as they approached, one slow movement at a time. Why did they move so slowly? Would I lose my mettle before they arrived?

My blood rushed in my ears as I tried to stay sharp, to be ready, to meet my death coming.

"Show yourself," I blustered, but my voice betrayed my fear.

When the light finally reached the boat, a spirit's voice, an echoing woman's voice, came out of the light from all directions. "Aodhan!" the voice said. "Aodhan."

My true name echoed all around me, and I knew for certain my death had come. I dropped the knife into the boat, and prayed, to all the gods I had been taught in the old country, to all the gods of the new.

"Aodhan," the voice said again, and then the light brightened, so painfully bright, until the whole world was red and I could hear nothing but the voice.

"He who passes here must face his greatest fear, or die," the voice said. And then the voice was gone, and I was alone in the red, in the terrible brightness.

I saw my mother die, again, in front of me, as our town burned, the enemy in their terrible helmets laying waste to all in front of them. My mother pushed me behind her skirts as I, six summers old, cowered. My master fought past her guards and killed her with one blow of his short sword. She fell, half on top of me, her gold-embroidered skirts hitting me with horrible force.

She wouldn't wake up. My whole being was overcome with the horror of my younger self at six summers. My mother wouldn't wake up! I felt it all over again, a crushing weight of sorrow, her blood staining her skirts— and me—as a huge fist came over to grab my shoulder. "You're mine now," the horrible monster said. "You'll do as I say."

In my mind, I ran and ran, but my master, then as now, clasped my six-summers-old self into chains and dragged me behind him. Soul-crushing pain washed over me, physical, pain of the heart and the head as well, as I fought helplessly against the inevitable.

But this was old pain, known pain, pain that had sat in my heart with a heavy weight for so many years I knew it like an old friend. This pain would not destroy me.

The memories disappeared, like wind blowing away fog, and the world turned green.

I smelled the fires of my homeland; I saw the villages that had birthed me ahead on the beach. But this time I—I was the enemy. My thick arms held a strong sword, bore up under leather armor. On my head were the horns of a warrior, and I would kill all who stood in my path.

Women ran from me, expressions of terror on their faces, and I saw a small boy. I lifted my sword—

And I pulled back, back. How I did not know, but I would not be the cause of a boy's death, nor of his mother's. I would not, even should it cause my own death. I would not.

The other warriors turned to me and called me names, horrible names, coward being the worst, coward being dark and deep and shameful in their tongue. One lifted an axe, and it came down on my skull—and the scene was gone.

I would die, from cowardice. I had always known it. I would always know it. I found myself back in the fog, unsure. Let the death come. I knew what I was.

I waited.

Nothing.

I waited longer, and finally cried, "Why tarry you, spirit? I am ready for my death. Only let it be quick. Only let it be quick, and I am ready."

But instead, the light faded and another scene opened, daylight this time in the same village, and I, alone, a traveler's pack on my back. I walked among my people, nodding, smiling, but they all turned away. I spoke to the people, but my voice came out rough, like the enemy's. They turned away, and the warriors came with swords to force me out.

I thought of fighting, of proving, but I could do nothing. Nothing at all. And so I turned, and walked away from my home, now a stranger.

I cried tears into the empty light, then. I could not, I could not return. I could not be what I was.

Into the empty light, void of all color, came a slow song then, a song in the key of my home. The voice sang it to me, and in the song came comfort. My heart shed its fear like a seabird shedding water, and I stood in the empty light. If this was death, I was no longer afeared.

I found myself back in the canoe, a mile from shore in the open sea, with a heavy pile of golden coins in my lap, a sword that shone with a dull green light in my right hand, and an oar lighter than a feather in the other.

I settled the sword next to my hip at the bottom of the canoe, noticing my knife was gone, and moved to paddle in to shore. My thin arms felt strong, new, capable of anything.

On the shore, the crowd stared as I pulled my canoe up onto the shore. Erik's mother huddled with his father, her shoulders shaking with tears she wouldn't let escape.

The priest stood, his ancient staff settled against the sand. I walked up to him, my head bowed as if against a blow.

"You are the last," the priest said.

After a long, long pause, he raised his hand and said the words that would make me a man, a warrior.

When he finished, he said: "The sea gives gold but seldom. Should you wish, you can become my apprentice."

I stared at him, not sure what to say.

"You have the life-price to buy your freedom from your master," he said finally, "and likely more, from the look."

I glanced back at Erik's parents.

"The boy was lost in the crossing," the priest said. "Some are weak, and some are not." He put his hand on my shoulder. "Sometimes the strength does not show. You are a man now, and you may do what you wish."

I stood, awkward, unsure of life itself in that moment. "I will think on this," I said. "I am grateful." I had not thought to apprentice with the priest, to sing and chant and usher the *sidr* through its phases to the good of the village. "I will think on this," I promised the priest, and I would.

I accepted a final blessing, and walked up the beach, the crowd parting in front of me. I stood tall, as a strong warrior would do, carrying my sword.

I could do what I wished.

The memory of myself on that beach in my homeland remained. Though I could do as I wished, there were some things I did not wish to do.

And maybe, today, I believe that did not make me a coward. Sometimes the strength does not show, as the priest said. The bag of gold was heavy in my hand, as heavy as the weight of the fears I'd shed.

Today I was a man, and free.

<<<<>>>>

Space Treasure
By Alex Hughes

Written from a Three Words prompt by reader Clarence W., *empty, throne, binary.*

The macrocrawler robot crept down the abandoned hallway of the Vaya starship in fits and starts, the servos on its light-treads struggling with every meter of distance. Its masters back on the base weren't willing to send any newer model on such a minor salvage operation.

The hallway was hexagonal, like all of the Vaya's. Honeycomb paneling covered every meter of the side walls, and some smaller panels on the top, now empty, where worker-drones had once lived close to their tasks.

The macrocrawler ran into something brittle that cracked and gave way. The crawler waited while its masters turned its one remaining functional camera to face the obstruction. When it finally saw, it wondered at its vision. Finally, its binary brain identified the shape: what had been a worker-drone Vaya, now decomposing in the middle of the hallway, its wings shredded, its carapace cracked, its internal organs turning to dust. The macrocrawler slowly backed up, its treads skipping, and turned, one shallow change at a time, until it could move around the drone's body. Its camera turned to watch as the body got further and further away.

At the end of the hallway opened a large space that tickled at the macrocrawler's on-again-off-again echolocation system, too large to easily read. The camera turned again, as the macrocrawler came to a careful, pre-programmed stop.

Slowly, the camera turned until it showed the throne, the mound of decomposing organics and wired machine that had been the Vaya queen—

once. The circle of control boards around her were long since stripped of their wired parts, her arms long since taken for their jeweled chitinous forms. The macrocrawler moved forward, slowly, its binary brain searching for the last location of the salvage.

Under the third panel, inside a gutted shell of what had been machine, the macrocrawler finally found it. The machine's one remaining grip-claw slowly extended, jerky and determined. Its pincer closed by increments, and it dropped the object.

The macrocrawler backed up, refocused on the treasured object, and this time gripped it firmly in its claws. Then, one difficult meter at a time, it made the halting journey back through the Vaya's ship to its home base.

On the other side of the airlock, a teenaged boy took off his headset and squatted down to examine the small robot. He looked around to make sure no one had seen him, and then took the worn action figure from the macrocrawler's pincer.

"Thanks, buddy," he said, and patted the macrocrawler's upper surface.

The binary brain inside examined the gesture, and considered its meaning. Finally, it came to the conclusion: it had done well. It was pleased.

The Bone Sculptures
By Alex Hughes

Inspired by a creepy dream. Written with a Three Words prompt by reader Susanne F., with the words *cupcake, curly horse,* and *death metal.*

I followed the tour group through the Dark Magic Artisans halls, past all the laboratories, some shown and some locked away, and even through the large auditorium where they played a propaganda film with upbeat music for the tourists. Black-iced cupcakes with tiny skulls and crossbones sat in the lobby, quickly gobbled up by the crowd. I refused them; I wasn't very hungry after seeing the death experiments, and anyway I was on a diet.

One of the guys next to me, a large man with a blond, shaggy beard, was probably in his thirties. He looked up when I stood next to him, but then returned his attention to the guide. The man was annoyingly out of place in a group of tourists; he had the skinny jeans of a much smaller man, and a T-shirt with a murder joke he probably thought was funny. What guys don't realize is that we don't like the bad boys as much as they think we do; females like the illusion of danger, sure, but the actuality of coming home to it every night turns you off real quick, and these days I wasn't even attracted to the illusion.

In the lobby, the tour guide was droning on about the wall hangings, made from the hides of curly horses. In his first few days on the job, he'd told the tourists the truth, that the hides had been taken while the horses were still alive, but several had thrown up and left the building, so he'd stopped telling them that.

The man seemed strangely attracted to the hangings, with an almost perverse glee, reaching out and touching them whenever he got near. From the feel, he was probably here hoping to apply to the Dark Magic school in the back. I probably should have warned him what he was getting into, but anybody with that kind of ambition deserves what they get.

There were maybe fifteen tourists around us, a slow day. Too many people came to the Artisans tour lately. Too many.

I sighed, and followed along. An infinity later, they exited the building through the side door, past the garden of bone sculptures.

The garden was a small place, stark, like the sand and rocks of a Zen garden, filled with bleached gravel and dead grass. Fifteen sculptures held places of honor in a semi-circle around a central one, the most important one. Whether the tourists knew it or not, a lot of the power of the Artisans was tied to this place.

The bone sculptures held an odd fascination for me, beauty and horror mixed. They were geometric lattices of overlapping bones, like the layered spirals you drew on paper, the bones bleached and carved in places, left with chunks of skin and cartilage in others. You could feel the blood still attached, the psychic residue of dark magic, the screaming of it through every mental sphere, but they were beautiful, fanning out patterns of bone with skin to hold the shape. They were beautiful in their terror, and terrible in their intricate beauty.

The tour guide explained that each sculpture was the master-project of a dark magician, sometimes two or three. Often, people willed their remains to be used in just such a project, for the beauty of it. Their souls would always be a part of a larger whole. Their energy always kept. They would never disappear.

Their souls would be harnessed to serve the goals of the Artisans, I thought but did not say.

"I'd like my bones to become part of this," the man said.

The tour guide smiled. "We will get you the paperwork as soon as the tour is complete."

Meanwhile, the tourists had gotten out their cameras and started taking pictures of the bone sculptures. The flash hit me, over and over, distracting, painful.

Then something strange happened. The man looked at me, and then at the bone sculpture in front of him. "I can feel it," he said, quietly, the pretense going out of his voice. He sounded as open and vulnerable as a child.

"Feel what?" one of the tourists asked, a young guy of about eighteen.

"The souls. They are all souls. The sculptures. Some have several."

"What?" a tourist asked him, sidling away.

"No, it's incredible." He went to his knees in front of one of the sculptures, the central, most important sculpture, and reached out a hand to touch the arch of bones.

I shivered.

"The soul." He took a breath. "Oh. This one isn't . . . she wasn't willing. She . . . she is a woman. A woman in her prime. She is angry, so angry. They stole her bones and she is angry. Her fury screams at me," he said.

I took a step back, panicking a little. He wasn't just a want-to-be, was he? He was a raw magician, someone with the sight, not just the inclination. Another Artisan. I took another step back, and then hit the limit. I was stuck; I could go no further. I fumed.

The man rubbed the arch of the bones, and anger rose in me. Bad enough that she was stuck there! Bad enough they so defiled her, must he touch the bones, too?

He looked up, directly at me. "They killed her. She is angry, and afraid. She doesn't want to see that she is dead."

"I am not dead," I hissed, and the wind blew through the garden, harsh. "And you will be soon if you join the Artisans."

"He has already promised. Now, enough of that." The tour guide raised his talisman, and the world shrunk into one, cold arch—a sculpture of bones, bone and spirit still in them.

I am angry, yes, and my anger will never be quenched. The Artisans . . . the Artisans . . . I felt a pulling on my soul, a shredding of my spirit.

The last thought trailed off until the next time, until the next time they let me go.

I would walk. I would.
I would not be dead.

BONUS STORY:

Cartoon Bastard Clouds
By Alex Hughes

This one was inspired from a lesson at the Odyssey Writing Workshop, where Jeanne Cavelos taught about "after the fact" stories, interesting scenes that happen after some huge event, where the point is to figure out what happened. I thought I'd try my hand at one, and see if it would make sense as a strict monologue. Here's the (very experimental) result.

I'm so sorry I'm late! Yes, yes, nice to meet you, too, thank you so much for waiting. Downtown traffic was so much . . . I meant Midtown, of course. Bumper to bumper. Surprised you didn't see it too. Bumper–to–bumper— really bad. Really.

Can I get you . . . oh, you already have coffee. No, no, I'm glad you didn't wait. . . . None for me. You wouldn't believe my day if I told you; the last thing I need is caffeine, trust me. Just give me a sec to put my purse down.

Well, like I said on the phone, Phoenix Gallery is . . . we're very well connected with the Inman Park crowd, yes. Very well connected. Why, just last week the mayor's wife came up to me and said. . . . No, of course not, I'm not saying that. But we're very well connected. Perfect for what you're talking about.

The finest artists, yes. Annalette Jackson has darling, kitschy pop art that's doing very well right now, and we have a pumpkin splatter artist coming in at the end of May. . . . Well, what do you need for the event? Like I said, we're very well connected. I'm sure one of our artists would be just perfect for what you need.

Landscapes. Well. They're a tad boring, don't you think? . . . Of course not. But the public loves what they know, and we can introduce them to plenty of. . . . Okay. I'll be honest with you, I'm sick to death of landscapes.

My bastard boyfriend was—is—a huge landscape painter. . . . The bastard cheated on me. I just found out yesterday. Yeah, it's the worst. And every time I see a cloudscape I think of him. It's disgusting.

He's a real bastard. . . . I didn't know that about you. I guess we have something in common. I agree; men are pigs.

But back to your event. We'd be happy to set it up for your organization. We'll invite half the city, get some lovely tapas. Invite the wine shop next door to take care of the booze. . . . No, you're right, totally nonalcoholic. So much classier that way.

I know a—wait. My violinist isn't available anymore. Sick. . . . Yes, that's right, she's sick. Very sick. Likely fatal. No, no, of course, I'm not wishing her dead or anything. I'm sure she'll pull through and be right as rain. I'm just saying we'll need to make other arrangements for the music. . . . I've never had a trumpet player in the gallery before. I've always been worried about the acoustics. . . . No, I'm sure we could make it work. We'll set up one of those noise shields so it doesn't get too loud.

Of course we'll give you prominent placement, a big sign right under our. . . . Well, okay, but we'd need a mention in your company . . . no, I agree it's great publicity. We'll iron out the details on both sides later.

Correct, but landscapes are so passé. Let's do something dark. Edgy, provocative. I'm picturing an installation with red splatters on tile, naked forms on crisp sheets, a stuffed panda bear. Maybe a chrysanthemum or two—they're always creepy. . . . Of course not; it's your event.

Green merchandising does sell well. Maybe recycled art? We have several artists on our books with that specialty. John Peters makes sculptures out of trash, for example a man constructed from sharpened kitchen knives.

Too violent, you're right. Fluffy bunnies and cartoon bastard clouds. Recycled plastic sounds like a great gig. . . . Absolutely. If they're there I'll find them. By Monday might be tough. . . . No, absolutely Friday at the latest. Next Friday. After I get a few things cleared away. I have a trip to run down to the lake house before I—

No, of course. You're my most important client. The company—you're right, a lot of rich art buyers. I'm very motivated. We'll do it on Friday the—

What? Something in my hair? No, no, it's—uh, paint, red paint. No big deal. Just a little project this afternoon, really a funny little thing. On my skirt too? Wow, that stuff gets everywhere. I washed, I swear, after I— changed clothes even. . . . No, it's just a stupid little thing. Quite funny. Very funny. . . . No, it's not a—you kinda had to be there. But the stuff gets everywhere, you know?

No, no, I completely understand. We'll work it out. Sorry I couldn't make it sooner.

You're not going to call anyone, are you?

<<<<>>>>

Sorry I Broke the Universe
by Alex Hughes

At Odyssey Writing Workshop in the last weeks, my roommates and I were sitting around, talking out of sheer exhaustion between writing sessions. One of us suggested that we all write a story with the same title and share them at the end of the week. We all agreed. Someone suggested "Sorry I Broke the Universe," and I was off to the races. Oddly enough, nobody else ended up writing a story with that title that week.

Marmon the hamster rolled in his ball through the streets of gold, past the crystal sea, and all the way up to the grand throne of the Almighty God. His hamster ball made plasticky sounds as he passed the mansions of the blessed. He paddled faster.

Near the throne, the cherubim sang in chorus, their thousand tiny wings ringing their faces of eyes. Suppliants and saints of every kind surrounded the throne, waiting their turns, worshipers throwing themselves on their faces all around. God was in a particularly shining mood today, the glory of his countenance lighting Heaven with a cheerful glory.

Marmon stopped by the administrative table, currently staffed by St. Paul. He opened the porthole in his hamster ball and squeaked up at Paul. "I have an emergency," he said. "Priority One."

"Death, disaster, or despair?" Paul said, assembling a stack of forms with arms that moved like lightning. He paused, waiting for the information for the last form.

"Disintegration," Marmon squeaked so quietly he had to repeat himself. "I made a mistake!" he said. "I need to see God now!"

St. Paul blinked at him. "Really, kid? Disintegration? After the big training moment last week? I thought we went over this."

"It's an emergency," Marmon said, his front paw coming up on the edge of the ball as his whiskers twitched. "Let me through. Now."

"Hold on, kid. There's paperwork. I need—"

"Do it for me." Marmon shook his head and pushed forward, moving the ball in one big jump as he tumbled around and around, running to staying on his feet.

The ball landed in a straight line towards the Throne. God stopped the ball with a foot. He waved the cherubim to a lower volume and picked Marmon's ball up gently.

Screwing up all of his courage, Marmon tripped the release to the ball's cap and poked his head out of the hole. God seemed patient, holding out a giant hand for Marmon to take the next step on his own.

Marmon, now shaking from the light of reflected glory–and the knowledge he'd screwed up big this time–eased out, paw by paw, until he was fully on God's hand.

Keeping Marmon at the level of his eyes, God put the hamster ball on His lap. "Why are you here?" God asked.

All around, disoriented worshipers poked their heads up to see what was going on. Some, at seeing the hamster in God's hands, scratched their heads and whispered to each other.

Terrified, Marmon buried his head beneath his paws. "You're God. You know already! I am a fool! I know it!"

God shrugged. "I'll need to explain the situation to most of the saints when you leave. It saves time this way. Besides, it's good for you to tell the truth."

"I'm so sorry!" Marmon squealed. "So sorry I broke the universe! The big red button just seemed so shiny sitting there. I had to push it. Now the black hole is eating the Epsilon Galaxy! The worlds are ending! I am so sorry! I gave in to temptation! I am a fool!"

God started to laugh, long booming laughs that shook the foundations of Heaven. The cherubim joined in with a babble of delight, and the saints, a full three beats behind, started tittering, not like they understood the joke, but like they'd rather not be left out.

Marmon trembled with fear. God was laughing at him. Smiting couldn't be far behind. His fur stood up in panicked clumps, and his little whiskers shook.

"Ah, Marmon," God said. "You are very precious. I forgive you, of course. I'm glad you understand what you did wrong."

"But the Epsilon! The black hole . . ."

"I know," God said. A flash of light came and a tiny roll of pink duct tape settled on God's other palm. "Here you go."

Marmon reached out his little paw delicately. "You want me to . . . ?"

"Well, you did break it," God said.

Marmon screwed up his courage and took the tape. He paddled his ball past the saints' mansions, past the crystal sea, and down the streets of gold. He would have to get directions to the Epsilon Galaxy. At least the duct tape roll was endless.

<<<<>>>>

Note From The Author

Thank you so much for reading! Readers like you make everything possible.

If you liked this book and want more, sign up for my email newsletter at http://www.ahugheswriter.com/email-signup. Newsletter subscribers receive information about new releases and sales, upcoming projects, and occasionally free reads!

Also check out my website and blog at http://www.ahugheswriter.com. On my site, you can read excerpts from all my work plus fun articles and interviews.

Also, please consider leaving a review of this book on the site where you purchased it or on a book review website. Reviews—both good and bad—mean the world to writers and help other readers decide if the book is right for them. Reviews don't have to be long or fancy; just a few words about how the book made you feel is perfect.

Thank you again for reading!

MINDSPACE INVESTIGATIONS

Rabbit Trick
Clean
Payoff
Sharp
Marked
Vacant
Fluid

OTHER WORKS

How To Drive Yourself Crazy As A Writer: A Modest Proposal for Wordsmiths

www.ingramcontent.com/pod-product-compliance
Lightning Source LLC
Chambersburg PA
CBHW020651130626
46552CB00003B/1495